To Emily
Happy Bir[thday]
Love n' Kisses
Donna, Steve
Coral & Aaron

D0526555

SONNY'S BIRTHDAY PRIZE

Text and illustration copyright © Lisa Stubbs, 1997

All rights reserved. No part of this publication may be reproduced, stored in a retrieval system, or transmitted, in any form or by any means electronic, mechanical, photocopying or otherwise, without prior permission of the copyright owner.

The right of Lisa Stubbs to be recognised as Author of this work has been asserted by her in accordance with the Copyright, Designs and Patents Act 1988.

Designed by Paul Cooper Design
Printed and bound in Belgium by Proost
for the publishers Piccadilly Press Ltd.,
5 Castle Road, London NW1 8PR

ISBN: 1 85340 422 5 (hardback)
1 85340 427 6 (paperback)

A catalogue record of this book is available from the British Library

Lisa Stubbs lives in Wakefield. She trained in Graphic Communications at Batley Art College and has illustrated greetings cards for a number of years. Her first book was SONNY'S WONDERFUL WELLIES, also published by Piccadilly Press.

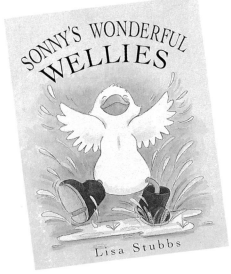

SONNY'S WONDERFUL WELLIES
ISBNs: 1 85340 369 5 (hardback)
1 85340 495 0 (paperback)

SONNY'S BIRTHDAY PRIZE

Lisa Stubbs

Piccadilly Press • London

When Sonny was leaving playgroup his friend Katie gave him an invitation to her birthday party on Saturday.

"Thank you," said Sonny.

As soon as he got home, Sonny made Katie a card. Gran had already knitted a scarf, which she wrapped up for Katie's present.

When Saturday came, Sonny was very excited. He eagerly washed his face and brushed his beak ready for Katie's party.

At the party, Sonny gave Katie her card and present. "They're brilliant," said Katie.

Sonny saw all her wonderful presents and wished that just one was for him.

They all sat down to a birthday tea. They ate banana sandwiches, jelly and ice cream. When Katie blew out the candles on the birthday cake, everyone sang "Happy Birthday".

After tea, Katie's dad
organised the party games.
They played Musical Statues . . .

Pin the Tail on the Donkey . . .

and Pass the Parcel.

Sonny was sad when he didn't
win any of the games.

Then they played Hide and
Seek. Katie started counting,
"1 . . . 2 . . . 3 . . . Coming,
ready or not."

"Found
you!"

"I can
see
you!"

It was soon time for the
children to go home. Katie had
found all of them – except Sonny.
"Where *is* Sonny?"
asked Grandma.

Everyone looked for Sonny while Katie's dad tidied up in the kitchen.

"He's here!" shouted Katie's dad,
pointing at the wash basket.

Sonny won first prize for
finding the best ever hiding place!